Abe Lincoln at Last!

Magic Tree House® Books

Merlin Missions

Magic Tree House® Fact Trackers

NEW!

More Magic Tree House®

GAMES AND PUZZLES FROM THE TREE HOUSE

MAGIC TREE HOUSE® #47
A MERLIN MISSION

Abe Lincoln at Last!

by Mary Pope Osborne

illustrated by Sal Murdocca

SCHOLASTIC INC.

ISBN 978-0-545-68949-6

12 11 10 9 8 7 6 5 4 3 2 1   15 16 17 18 19/0

Printed in the U.S.A.   40

First Scholastic printing, January 2014

For Mary Sams

CONTENTS

Not often in the story of mankind does a man arrive on earth who is both steel and velvet, who is hard as rock and soft as drifting fog. . . .
—Carl Sandburg

Prologue

One summer day in Frog Creek, Pennsylvania, a mysterious tree house appeared in the woods. A brother and sister named Jack and Annie soon learned that the tree house was magic—it could take them to any time and any place in history.

Jack and Annie have since gone on many adventures in the magic tree house and have completed many missions for both Morgan le Fay and Merlin the magician of Camelot. On some of their journeys, Jack and Annie have received help from two young enchanters, Teddy and Kathleen, who are learning magic from Merlin and Morgan.

Now Teddy is in big trouble. While Merlin and Morgan were away, Teddy accidentally put a spell on Penny, Merlin's beloved penguin. The spell turned her into a stone statue. Teddy thinks that he could be banished from the kingdom—unless Jack and Annie can help!

Teddy and Kathleen have found an ancient spell that can undo Teddy's accidental magic. To make the ancient spell work, Jack and Annie must find four special things—each from a different time and place. They have already found two of these things: an emerald in the shape of a rose and a white and yellow flower.

Now Jack and Annie are waiting to find out what they must search for next. . . .

CHAPTER ONE

The Third Thing

Annie peeked into Jack's room.

"Ready?" she whispered.

"Yep," said Jack.

Even though it was two hours before school started, Jack and Annie were already dressed. Jack put his notebook and pencil into his backpack. Then he picked up the pack and his sneakers and followed Annie into the hall. In their sock feet, Jack and Annie tiptoed past their parents' bedroom. Then they slipped down the stairs.

When they reached the front hall, Jack and

Annie put on their jackets and shoes and stepped outside. The early-morning sky was gray. Everything was quiet, except for the sound of a gentle spring rain.

"Should we get our raincoats?" Jack asked.

"It's clearing up," said Annie. She pointed to blue sky in the distance.

"Oh, good," said Jack. "Let's hurry."

Jack and Annie stepped off their porch. Then they ran up the sidewalk and crossed the street. By the time they started into the Frog Creek woods, the rain had stopped. Misty rays of sunlight slanted down through the wet trees.

Jack and Annie kept going until they came to the tallest oak. The leaves at the top of the tree sparkled with raindrops, and the magic tree house was lit by the morning sun.

"It's waiting for us," said Jack.

"I knew it would be," said Annie. She grabbed the rope ladder and started up.

Jack climbed after her. Inside the tree house,

they looked around for the two special things they had found on their last missions.

"Great, they're still here," said Jack, pointing to a green jewel and a white and yellow flower in the corner.

"And it looks like Teddy and Kathleen sent some stuff for us," said Annie.

Lying in the shadows was a book. Next to it were a small folded note and a tiny blue bottle. Jack picked up the book. Its cover showed an old black-and-white photograph of a building. It looked like the White House in Washington, D.C.

Jack gasped. "Oh, man! Abraham Lincoln!"

THE LIFE OF ABRAHAM LINCOLN

"Wow," said Annie, looking at the book's cover. "He was a great president."

"No kidding," said Jack. "Do you think we're actually going to meet him?" He opened the book to the first page and read aloud:

Abraham Lincoln served as president of the United States from March 1861 until his assassination in April 1865. He led the country through the terrible crisis of the American Civil War. He preserved the union of states and outlawed slavery.

"I can't believe it," Jack said, closing the book. "Abraham Lincoln! Do you think *he's* supposed to help us find the third thing to break the spell that turned Penny into a statue?"

"Maybe," said Annie. "Let's see what else Teddy and Kathleen left for us. . . ." She picked up the tiny bottle and the note. She unfolded the note and read aloud:

*The third thing to break the spell
is a single feather from a hero's hand.
Use it wisely to give him hope—
the hope he needs to heal his land.*

"That sounds like a riddle," said Jack.

"I'll bet Abraham Lincoln is the hero," said Annie. "And"—she looked at the note again—"we have to get a feather from him. Then we'll use the feather to give him hope."

"Confusing," said Jack.

"A lot of our missions sound confusing at first, don't you think?" said Annie. "But in the end, they all make sense."

"Yeah, I guess," said Jack. "But that doesn't help us right now. There must be a magic potion in the bottle. What does the label say?"

Annie held up the small blue bottle and read the tiny writing on its label aloud:

Take a sip. Make a wish for <u>one thing</u> to help you on your mission. Remember: Trust the magic.

"That sounds kind of general," said Jack. "Wish for one thing to help us on our mission? That could be *anything*."

"And remember to trust the magic," said Annie. She shrugged.

"Okay . . . we'll try to do that," said Jack. He took the bottle and the note from Annie and put them into his backpack.

"We've got everything we need," said Annie. "A mission, a research book, and a little bit of magic. Ready to go?"

"Yep," said Jack. He pointed to the picture of the White House on the cover of their book and said, "I wish we could go there!"

The wind started to blow.

The tree house started to spin.

It spun faster and faster.

Then everything was still.

Absolutely still.

CHAPTER TWO

Pirate Captain

Jack shivered. The air was chilly, but the sun was bright. Bare branches outside the tree house swayed in the wind. Annie was wearing a long dress with an apron. Jack wore a cotton shirt over a red undershirt and a pair of trousers with suspenders. His backpack had turned into a leather bag.

Jack looked into the bag. Inside were his notebook and pencil, the message from Teddy and Kathleen, and the bottle with the magic potion. "Good," he said, "it's all here."

"We've worn clothes like these before," said Annie.

"Yeah, when we ran from that twister on the prairie," said Jack.

"And when we helped Clara Barton in the Civil War," said Annie.

"Right," said Jack. "So, did we land at the White House?"

They looked out the window. The tree house had landed in a grove of bare, sunlit trees. Beyond the trees, horse-drawn carriages rumbled over a circular carriageway toward a stately white mansion with tall columns.

"Oh, man," whispered Jack.

The White House was breathtaking in the morning air, bathed in sunlight. A crowd was gathered outside the front entrance: men in long black coats and tall hats, and women in hoopskirts and bonnets with big bows.

"Looks like lots of people are visiting Abraham Lincoln today," said Annie.

Jack thumbed through their research book until he found another black-and-white photograph of the White House. He read aloud:

When Abraham Lincoln became president in 1861, the White House was considered to belong to all the citizens of the country, as well as to the president and his family. Anyone could walk right

in. President Lincoln sometimes found
it hard to work in his White House
office because of the number of people
swarming through the building.

"So *anyone* can just walk right into the White
House and look for the president?" said Annie.

"That's crazy," said Jack.

"But it's good for us!" said Annie.

"I guess," said Jack, "but I don't want to be
one of those people who make it hard for the president to work."

"Don't forget," said Annie, "we're supposed to
give him hope."

"With a feather that *he's* supposed to give *us*,"
said Jack. He shook his head, then took out their
note from Teddy and Kathleen.

The third thing to break the spell
is a single feather from a hero's hand.
Use it wisely to give him hope—
the hope he needs to heal his land.

"How can we get a feather from him?" said Jack. "And how can it give him hope?"

"It's better to do just one thing at a time," said Annie. "First we have to find the president."

"Hey, Willie! Look!" someone shouted from below. "It's a tree house! See? See?"

"Oh, no!" whispered Jack.

Jack and Annie peeked out the window. A boy about seven or eight years old was looking up at the tree house. The boy wore baggy gray trousers with suspenders and a white shirt. He had dark, piercing eyes.

"Hello!" the boy shouted when he saw Jack and Annie. "Who are you? Why are you in our tree house?"

"*Your* tree house?" said Jack. "It's not your tree house!"

"Yes, it is!" the boy said confidently.

"Tad, hush!" An older boy ran to join the younger one. He had a friendly, open smile and looked to be around Jack's age. "Don't mind my brother Tad!" he shouted.

"But it's *ours,* Willie!" said Tad. "The White House is our house! And the tree house is in *our* yard!"

Oh, man, thought Jack. That was what the book said, too: the White House was considered to belong to all the citizens of the country, as well as to the president.

"I'm sorry, but this tree house is not like the White House," Jack called. "It doesn't belong to the citizens of the country. It's ours!"

"No, it's not!" yelled Tad. "I'm coming up!"

"No, you're not!" Jack yelled back. He reached for the rope ladder to pull it up. But Tad had already started climbing.

"Hide our stuff!" Jack said to Annie.

Jack quickly pushed the Lincoln book into his leather bag. Annie stuck their note and the tiny bottle into her apron pocket.

"Tad, come back!" called Willie. "Leave them alone!"

Tad scrambled into the tree house. He grinned at Jack and Annie, his dark eyes gleaming. "I'm a pirate captain, and I'm taking over your ship!" Tad shook his small fists in Jack's face. "Fight me!" he shouted.

"Cut it out," said Jack, waving him away.

"Tad!" Willie shouted from below.

The boy just laughed like a maniac and danced around the tree house, trying to box with Jack. "This is my ship now, matey!"

"Quit it!" said Jack.

"Tad!" his brother yelled again.

"Your brother's calling you," Annie said firmly to Tad. "Go! Now!"

"Who are you to boss me, missy?" Tad said, jutting out his chin.

Annie laughed. "I'm not a *missy*, shrimp," she said. "I'm Annie. And this is my brother, Jack."

Tad lowered his fists. "Oh! Hello, Annie, I'm Tad." He put out his hand, and Annie shook it. "Pleased to meet you," said Tad, completely dropping his role as pirate captain. "What are you and Jack doing today?"

"Actually, we're hoping to meet with President Lincoln," Annie said.

"Really?" said Tad. "Me and Willie know a

secret. . . ." He gave them a sly grin. "If you come with us, we'll take you straight to the president. I give you my word."

"Thanks, but we can handle it ourselves," said Jack. The last thing he wanted was for this kid to get in their way.

"But I *want* to help you. Come with me," said Tad. He started down the ladder.

"Should we go with him?" Annie whispered.

"No, he's just making stuff up," said Jack.

"Are you coming down?" called Tad. "Or should I come back up so we can play?"

"Darn," said Jack under his breath. "Let's go, just to get him away from the tree house." Jack grabbed his bag.

Suddenly Tad poked his head back into the tree house. "Are you coming or not?" he said.

"Yes! Go!" said Annie.

"What's in your bag?" asked Tad.

"Nothing," said Jack. "Go back down!" He didn't want Tad to see their Lincoln book.

"Let me see," said Tad, climbing into the tree house again. "What's inside?"

"Nothing, he told you nothing," said Annie.

"Then why is he bringing it with him?" Tad asked her.

"Fine, I'll leave it!" Jack said crossly. He dropped the leather bag to the floor. "Happy? Let's go!"

"Yes! Let's go!" said Tad, and he disappeared down the ladder again.

Jack reached into his bag, grabbed his small notebook and pencil, and stuck them into the back pocket of his pants. "I'll come back later and get the book," Jack whispered, "after we get rid of this kid."

Annie smiled. "If we can," she said. Then she and Jack started down the rope ladder.

CHAPTER THREE

Hide! Hide!

Willie was waiting at the bottom of the ladder. "Hello," he said.

"Willie, this is Jack and Annie," said Tad. "I told them that you and I have a secret." He gave Willie a meaningful look. "I told them we'd take them to meet the president. I gave them my word."

"Oh, you did, did you?" said Willie. "Hello, Jack and Annie." He shook hands with them. "I apologize for Tad," he added. "My brother is very high-spirited."

"And Willie's sweet as pie," said Tad, making a face. "Come on, you all! To the White House!" He saluted, then took huge marching steps across the lawn.

"So does Tad really know the president?" Annie asked as she and Jack walked with Willie.

"He does," said Willie with a smile, "and so do I."

"Oh. Cool," said Jack. He liked Willie's kind, mature manner. He wouldn't mind if *Willie* introduced them to the president. "Do you think you could introduce us?"

"If Tad doesn't introduce you first," said Willie, "then I'd be happy to."

"That would be great," said Jack.

As Tad marched ahead of them, Jack, Annie, and Willie walked through the sun-dappled grove of trees. The air was chilly, but it smelled like spring. It looked like spring, too. Tiny buds sprouted from bare branches. Birds flitted from tree to tree, and robins hunted for worms in the green grass.

"Are your parents visiting the White House today?" Annie asked Willie.

"You could say that," said Willie.

"Look at me!" Tad called. He was running backward up the carriageway.

"Watch out, Tad!" shouted Willie.

Tad jumped out of the path of a horse-drawn carriage just in time. The carriage stopped in front of the president's house. The crowd was huge now. As people tried to squeeze through the front doors, some waved pieces of paper at the guard.

"Everyone wants to meet the new president!" said Tad. "They all want something from him."

"Don't talk that way, Tad," said Willie. He turned to Jack and Annie. "They're mostly looking for jobs in the government. They have to take care of their families."

Tad led the way past the carriages and between the columns to the crowd at the door. "Allow us to enter!" he shouted to the guard at the door. "Jack and Annie are here! Important friends of the president!"

To Jack's amazement, the guard did as Tad

commanded. The man moved people aside and let Tad, Willie, Annie, and Jack walk right into the White House!

Jack trailed behind as they all passed through the entranceway. From there, they went around a bronze screen and into a wide hall filled with grown-ups.

"Make way!" shouted Tad as he squeezed through the crowd. A few women squealed. Their hoopskirts rocked and swirled.

"Stop, Tad!" said Willie, grabbing his brother. "Calm yourself!"

No kidding! thought Jack. He liked Willie a lot, but Tad was too wild and unpredictable.

Tad laughed and broke loose from his big brother. He ran into a room off the hallway. Willie and Annie hurried after him. A moment later, Jack heard someone banging on a piano.

Jack followed cautiously. He went through a door into a huge parlor filled with women and girls sipping tea from china cups.

The room had furniture covered in red satin. There was a large portrait of George Washington on the wall by the tall windows. No one was paying any attention to Tad as he pounded away on the piano keys. Even Willie was ignoring him. He was busy introducing Annie to a plump, dark-haired woman sitting on a sofa.

Abe Lincoln at Last!

Why don't the grown-ups stop this bratty kid?
Jack wondered. *Where are his parents? The White
House guards? The Secret Service?*

Tad turned his head and caught Jack frowning
at him. He jumped up from the piano bench,
rushed over, and grabbed Jack's hand. "Sorry,
mate! I almost forgot! I gave you my word!" he
said. "Come along!"

Jack tried to free himself from Tad as the boy pulled him out of the parlor.

"Stop! Let me go! I have to wait for my sister," said Jack. He looked back and saw Willie and Annie still talking with the woman on the sofa.

"They'll catch up to us," said Tad. "Come along! I have a secret that you won't believe!"

"Please! Leave me alone!" said Jack.

"No! Come with me, or I'll start screaming," said Tad. "And I can scream very, very loud." He had a wild look in his eye.

Oh, no! Jack thought. This kid was totally insane. "Don't scream, don't scream, just hold on a second." He called out, "Annie! Willie!" But neither of them looked up.

"C'mon! It's now or never!" said Tad. He pulled Jack down the carpeted hallway, toward a wide staircase.

"Let go! Let go of me! I'm serious!" Jack said.

Tad let go of him. "Please, please, come up the stairs with me," he begged. "If you don't, I'll . . ." He opened his mouth wide.

"Fine! I'll come!" Jack said through his teeth. He let Tad pull him through a group of grown-ups climbing the stairs. *When we get to the top, I'll run back down,* Jack thought. *Then he can scream as loud as he wants.*

As soon as they reached the hallway on the second floor, Jack turned around to run. But the stairway was packed with too many people to escape!

Tad grabbed Jack by the arm and pulled him to a door off the hall. "The president is right in there, I promise," he whispered. "Do you want to meet him? Or not?"

"Not," said Jack. *At least not with you,* he thought.

"But you said you did!" said Tad. He threw open the door and pulled Jack inside, then closed the door behind them.

Jack looked around. The room was empty of people. It had a huge wooden bed with purple drapes. Flying birds were carved into the black wood.

This must be the president's bedroom! Jack thought with awe and horror. He whirled around, but Tad gripped the door handle.

"We can't stay here, Tad," Jack whispered furiously. "We'll get in terrible trouble!"

"But President Lincoln is there, in his dressing room!" said Tad. He grinned, pointing to a closed door off the bedroom. "I told you I'd take you to him!"

"You are crazy," Jack whispered. "Move! I'm leaving! Before we get caught!"

Suddenly Tad groaned and fell to the floor.

"Tad?" said Jack. He bent down to check on him. "Tad, are you—"

Tad grabbed Jack's arm and pulled him to the floor, just as the dressing room door opened!

"Hide! Hide!" Tad whispered. He scrambled under the big wooden bed. Jack frantically crawled after him.

Jack held his breath as they lay on their stomachs under the bed. His heart was beating so hard that he thought he was going to have a heart attack! Tad covered his mouth and shook with silent laughter.

Two large feet in black socks stopped beside the bed. Jack felt the bed sink down. A pair of hands put a pair of large leather shoes down on the floor. The feet slipped into the shoes. Then the weight lifted off the bed, and the shoes stepped forward.

Tad crawled silently out from under the bed. Then he tackled the person wearing the shoes! The man yelled and fell to the floor. Tad sat on top of him and beat him with his small fists.

From his hiding place, Jack could see a dark-haired man lying on his side, groaning and moaning. Tad was attacking the president of the United States!

CHAPTER FOUR

Willie!

Jack was horrified. Would the Secret Service arrest him along with Tad? Jack had to stop him!

Suddenly the president burst out laughing. He wrapped his hands around Tad's fists. "You little tadpole," he said. "You didn't scare me one bit!" Then he started to tickle Tad.

"Pa, don't! Don't, Pa, don't!" Tad screamed and giggled and kicked.

Pa? Pa? Jack thought. *Abraham Lincoln is Tad's "pa"!*

The president laughed. He stopped tickling Tad and kissed the top of his head. "What are you doing in here, my boy?" he said.

"Pa, me and Willie found a tree house," said Tad. "Did you know there was a tree house here? Two kids were in it. Jack and Annie. Jack said it belonged to them. I told him it was mine because it's in our yard. Isn't it mine, Pa?"

Jack wanted to shout, *No, it's ours!* But he was afraid to be caught under the bed.

"Wait—what did you say their names were?" the president asked, sounding serious. "Jack and Annie?"

"Yes," said Tad. "They came out of nowhere. Don't you think the tree house is mine, Pa? Mine and Willie's?"

"They came out of nowhere?" said the president. "And their names are Jack and Annie? Are you sure?"

Why doesn't Tad tell him I'm right here— under the bed? Jack wondered. *Should I just crawl out?*

"Yes, Pa, Jack and Annie," said Tad. "But I want to know about the tree house. Do—"

The door opened. "Mr. President, you must come at once," a man said briskly. "You are late for your first meeting."

"Sorry, Mr. Nicolay," President Lincoln said. "I'll be right there." He stood up.

"The crowd is growing restless, sir," Mr. Nicolay said. "Before you know it, they'll storm your bedroom."

"Oh, they wouldn't dare," said the president, chuckling. "Not with my bodyguard here." He ruffled Tad's hair. "Come along, tadpole. Escort me to my new office down the hall."

"But when will you come and see the tree house, Pa?" Tad said as they started out of the door.

"Perhaps when I take my horseback ride later," the president said. "I'd like to meet this Jack and Annie." The door closed. And the room was quiet.

Tad forgot about me! Jack thought. He couldn't

believe it! Then he realized he'd better get out of the president's bedroom. He started to crawl out from under the bed, but the door opened again, so he quickly crawled back.

"Dust first?" Jack heard a girl say.

"Aye, then shake out the pillows and change the linens," said another.

Jack could only see the black stockings and shoes of the two maids as they bustled around the room. *Now,* he thought, *before they make the bed!* He scrambled out and ran to the door.

One of the girls screamed. Jack didn't look back. He threw open the door and headed for the stairs. As he bounded down the steps, one of the maids shrieked, "There was a boy under the bed!"

Jack reached the bottom of the stairs and squeezed through the crowd until he found a nook off the hallway. He scrunched against the wall, then peeked around the corner to see if anyone was coming after him.

Someone grabbed his arm.

"Ahh!" Jack yelled.

"It's me!" said Annie. "Where have you been? I've been looking all over for you!"

"I was upstairs! In President Lincoln's bed-room!" Jack said. "Tad made me go in there! Did you know that President Lincoln is Tad and Willie's dad?"

"That's what I was going to tell you. Willie introduced me to their mom!" said Annie. "She was really nice. Those were all her relatives in the parlor."

"Well, Tad tricked me into hiding under the bed, and I almost got caught!" Jack said. "And Tad didn't even remember I was there. He kept talking about the tree house, saying it was *his*."

"Willie says Tad gets overly excited," said Annie. "He can't help it. Plus, it's their very first week in the White House."

"Well, it was awful," said Jack. "I was trapped under the president's bed!"

Annie giggled. "You know, that's actually pretty funny," she said.

"Not really," said Jack.

"Don't worry," said Annie. "Willie would have saved you. He told me to find you and then come upstairs to his dad's office and he'll introduce us. It's on the second floor at the end of the hall."

"Okay," said Jack, sighing. "I heard the president say he'd like to meet us."

"Really?" said Annie.

"Yep, when Tad told him about the tree house and you and me, the president kept saying, 'Jack and Annie? Jack and Annie? Are you sure their names are Jack and Annie?'"

"That's weird," said Annie. "But I'm glad he wants to meet us. Come on."

Jack and Annie headed down the hallway and up the stairs. On the second floor, Jack kept his head down, just in case the maids were looking for him. Jack followed Annie down the hall toward a group of people standing outside a door.

A skinny man with a small pointed beard was speaking to them. "Ladies and gentlemen, please! I'm sorry, but only the names on my list can meet with the president today!"

Jack recognized the man's voice. "That's Mr. Nicolay," he told Annie.

"Who are you to tell us we can't see the president?" a woman in a pink bonnet asked Mr. Nicolay.

"I am President Lincoln's secretary, ma'am," Mr. Nicolay said sourly, "and if you do not have an appointment, you must leave."

"Excuse me, Mr. Nicolay, but I believe that I am on your list," said a dignified man. He showed the secretary a piece of paper. The secretary checked the paper against his list.

"Of course. This way, Mr. Bennet," Mr. Nicolay said. He opened the door and nodded for Mr. Bennet to enter, then followed him inside. While the door was open, Jack and Annie peeked into the room.

Abraham Lincoln was sitting at a long table. Tad was perched on his lap, fiddling with his dad's tie. Willie was studying a map on the wall, while

the president was listening to one of the men at the table.

"Willie!" Annie whispered loudly.

Willie didn't hear, but Mr. Nicolay did—he rushed back out of the president's office.

"Willie!" Annie shouted.

Willie turned around just as Mr. Nicolay closed the door.

CHAPTER FIVE

Leave Now!

"Excuse me, young lady!" Mr. Nicolay said. "This is not a time for play."

"I'm not playing, sir," said Annie as she and Jack stood at the front of the crowd. "We're friends of Tad and Willie's, and Willie just told us to come here to the president's office. He wants to introduce us to his dad."

Mr. Nicolay scowled. "I'm afraid Mr. Willie misspoke. The president does not have time to meet you now," he said. "He is in a private

meeting with delegates from California, Indiana, and Maine."

"Maybe later, then?" said Annie.

"Not maybe later," said Mr. Nicolay. "After this meeting he is scheduled to have a meeting with his generals, and then a meeting with the Department of the Navy."

"Excuse me—" a man in the crowd called out.

"But I heard the president say he'd like to meet us!" Jack broke in.

"I can't imagine why he said that," said Mr. Nicolay, shaking his head. "Following all the meetings I just listed, President Lincoln will meet with foreign diplomats, then with a group of senators, and then with reporters from the *New York Times.*"

"Mr. Nicolay! Listen to me!" someone shouted.

"So, sir," Annie interrupted, "you're saying he'll have no free time at all today?"

"Oh, he might have a free moment," said Mr. Nicolay. "But should that miracle occur, the president will go for a horseback ride in the country—and have a private meeting with himself!"

"Got it," said Annie. She took a deep breath. "Well, maybe you can just answer one question for us. Do you know if the president collects feathers?"

Mr. Nicolay threw up his hands. "This is no time for silly questions," he said. "Our country is divided, young lady. We are on the brink of war."

"What do you mean, sir?" one of the men in the crowd shouted. "What's the news from Fort Sumter?"

"Yes! What do you know that we don't know?" a lady called.

Everyone started shouting at once.

"That's it! Leave now, everyone!" Mr. Nicolay said. "The president is busy! He works night and day for you and for the unity of this nation!"

As the crowd shouted back at the secretary, Jack tugged on Annie's sleeve. "Let's get out of here," he said.

"We should wait for Willie," said Annie.

"I don't think Willie can help us," said Jack. "Come on. Let's go back to the tree house and look at our research book. Maybe we can think of something else."

"Okay," said Annie, sighing.

She and Jack hurried along the hallway, then down the stairs to the first floor. They wove through the crowd, then escaped out the main door.

"Phew! That place is nuts!" said Jack as they walked between the tall white columns of the White House.

"Are you sure we shouldn't wait for Willie?" said Annie.

"I'm sure," said Jack. He hurried down the carriageway. "Even if Willie took us back to the office to meet his dad, we wouldn't be alone with the president. Lots of other people would be there, too. We couldn't ask him for a feather. And we sure couldn't give him any hope. Everyone would laugh."

"You're right," said Annie.

Jack shook his head. "How can the president

even think in that place, with Tad jumping on him, his relatives visiting, his secretary yelling—"

"And a thousand people scheduled to meet with him," said Annie.

"And another thousand who are *trying* to meet with him!" said Jack.

They had arrived back at the tree house. "Whew. No wonder the president needs to take a ride in the countryside by himself," Jack said. He grabbed the sides of the ladder. "Let's go up and look at the book."

"Wait," said Annie. "I have a good idea."

"What?" asked Jack.

"Right now we really need to have our own meeting with Abraham Lincoln, alone," said Annie. "Right?"

"Yes . . . so?" said Jack.

"So if that's the one thing we need, our book can't really help," said Annie. "But I know something that *can*."

"What?" said Jack.

Annie reached into her apron pocket. She pulled

out the bottle and read the label aloud: "'Take a sip. Make a wish for *one thing* to help you on your mission. Remember: Trust the magic.'"

Annie looked up at Jack. "So why don't we make a wish to have a private meeting with Abraham Lincoln?"

"Isn't it too soon to use our only magic?" said Jack.

"Maybe. But maybe it's the perfect time," said Annie.

"So we wish to have a meeting with the president all by ourselves?" said Jack.

"Yep," said Annie.

Jack couldn't think of another plan. "Well . . . okay," he said. "Let's do it."

"Just remember, we have to trust the magic," said Annie.

Jack nodded.

Annie took the top off the bottle. She raised the bottle to her lips, then swallowed a quick sip of the potion. She handed the bottle to Jack, and he did the same.

"You can make our wish," said Annie.

Jack squeezed his eyes shut. "We wish to have a meeting with Abraham Lincoln!" he said. "Alone!"

There was a deafening *WHOOSH* and a *ROAR*. The earth shook, like a speeding train passing by. The ground opened, and Jack felt as if he were falling through space,

through a tunnel,

down through blackness,

into a world of daylight.

CHAPTER SIX

Trust the Magic

Clouds hid the sun. Jack and Annie sat in a clump of dead weeds beside a dirt road in the countryside. A chilly wind blew the creaky limbs of bare trees.

"You okay?" asked Annie.

"I think so," said Jack. "Where are we?"

"Looks like we're somewhere in the country," said Annie.

"No kidding, but where? Why?" said Jack.

"Wait, wait," said Annie. "Mr. Nicolay said if the president had a free moment, he'd take a ride in the country. I'll bet we've come to a spot where we can catch Abraham Lincoln on his ride! Alone!"

"Oh, wow . . . cool," said Jack.

"Look!" said Annie. "Someone's coming this way now! On a horse!"

A slim figure on a horse was coming down the dirt road. Jack and Annie jumped to their feet. When the rider on the bony white horse got closer, Jack sighed. "It's not the president," he said. "It's just some kid on an old horse."

"Maybe this kid is supposed to help us somehow," said Annie. "Remember, *trust the magic.*"

Jack nodded, but he couldn't imagine the boy would be much help. He looked to be ten or maybe eleven years old. His matted black hair stuck out from under a coonskin cap. His thin face was dirty, and his buckskin pants and moccasins were stained and torn. A frayed burlap sack hung from his shoulder.

Annie stepped into the road and waved. "Hello!" she called.

The boy pulled the old horse to a halt. He took off his cap and bowed his head. Then he put his cap back on and looked at them with tired gray eyes. "How do?" he said without a smile.

"We do good," said Annie. "We're wondering if you can help us. We're looking for Abraham Lincoln. Does he ride his horse around here? Have you ever seen him?"

The boy's eyes brightened. "You're looking for Abraham Lincoln?" he asked.

"Yes, we are," said Jack.

"Why?" the boy asked.

"Um . . . well, we just want to say hi to him," said Jack. "Do you know if he goes riding in this area?"

The boy nodded. "He does," he said. "In fact, he is in this area as we speak."

"Really?" said Annie. She smiled at Jack, as if to say, *See! The magic's working!*

Jack couldn't help smiling back. "So, can you tell us where we can find him?" he asked the boy.

"Yes," said the boy, nodding. "But I think it's better if I take you to him myself. I just have to grind some corn at the mill first."

How long will that take? Jack wondered. *How*

long will the president be riding in the country-side?

"Maybe you could just tell us where we could find him," said Jack. "We don't have much time."

"Wait," said Annie. She whispered to Jack, "We have to trust the magic."

Jack sighed. He looked back at the boy. "Okay, we'll go to the mill with you," he said, "but it would be good if we could hurry, so we don't miss finding Abraham Lincoln."

"You won't miss him. I give you my word," said the boy. "Come along. The grinder's around the bend. Giddyup, girl." He shook his reins, and the old horse started plodding down the road again.

Jack and Annie walked after the slow-moving horse. "Our names are Jack and Annie," Annie called. "What's yours?"

"You can call me Sam," the boy said over his shoulder.

"Okay, Sam," said Annie. "Thanks for helping us."

A gust of wind stirred the branches of the trees. The old horse neighed and stopped. "Keep going, girl," said Sam.

But the horse wouldn't budge.

"She doesn't hear well. She gets spooked by the wind," Sam explained to Jack and Annie.

The lonely sound of the wind spooked Jack, too. Something felt wrong. This weather was different from the weather at the White House.

"Giddyup, girl!" said Sam.

The horse started plodding down the road again. When they rounded the bend, Jack saw a strange-looking machine in a clearing. It had a barrel-like container with a wooden beam attached to it. Metal rods hung from the end of the beam.

"What's that?" said Jack.

"The grinder," said Sam. "You ain't never seen one before?"

"Sure, we have," said Annie.

No one was tending the grinder or waiting to use it. Sam dropped his sack to the ground and dismounted. He was tall and skinny. His buckskin pants were too short for him.

"What's in your bag?" asked Annie.

"Twenty pounds of corn," Sam said. "Shelled it all by hand."

"Wow," said Annie.

Sam poured the corn kernels into a funnel over the barrel. Then he hitched his old horse to leather straps attached to the metal rods.

Jack and Annie stood to the side and watched Sam walk his horse around in a circle. After a while, Jack grew impatient. The corn grinding seemed to be taking forever. Before he could say anything, though, a gust of wind came up and the horse reared.

"Keep moving, girl!" said Sam.

The horse neighed and tossed her head.

"Go on, girl! Giddyup!" said Sam. He slapped her backside. "Giddyup, I said!"

The horse didn't budge.

"These nice folks are waitin' on us!" said Sam. He pushed the horse from behind.

The wind picked up, tossing dead leaves into

the air. The horse neighed again, then kicked out with her hind foot. Her hoof hit Sam in the head! His coonskin cap flew off as he fell backward and sprawled across the ground.

"Sam!" cried Annie.

Annie and Jack knelt in the dirt beside the boy.

A trickle of blood ran down the side of his head. His eyes were closed.

"Sam?" said Annie. "Can you hear me?" She wiped the blood with her apron.

Sam didn't answer or open his eyes.

"Hey, Sam!" Jack said loudly. "Wake up!"

But Sam didn't move. He didn't even seem to be breathing.

Jack and Annie looked at each other.

"Is he dead?" whispered Annie.

CHAPTER SEVEN

Sam's Farm

"I don't know," said Jack. This was one of the worst things that had ever happened. He pressed his finger against Sam's wrist to feel for his pulse, like he'd seen on TV and in movies.

Sam's eyes opened. "Giddyup," he said weakly.

Jack laughed with relief. "Whew, we were afraid you were dead!" he said.

"Ain't dead yet," Sam whispered, blinking, "but I am seeing stars and my ears are ringing."

"Does your head hurt?" asked Annie.

"Yes, bad," Sam said quietly, his eyes squinting with pain.

"You might have a concussion," Jack said. "Is there a doctor nearby?"

"Thirty-five . . . ," said Sam.

"Minutes?" asked Jack.

"Miles," Sam whispered.

"Whoa, that's really far," said Annie.

"I have to go home . . . to our farm," said Sam. He struggled to sit up.

"Careful," said Jack. He couldn't remember what to do if someone had a concussion.

With Jack and Annie's help, Sam managed to get on his feet. "Thanks," the boy said. He staggered toward his horse, then swayed and collapsed onto the ground again.

"Sam!" said Annie. She and Jack gently helped him back up to a standing position.

"Dizzy . . . just dizzy," whispered Sam.

"We'll help you get home," said Annie. "You can't do it by yourself. Right, Jack?"

"Right," said Jack. He knew it was the right thing to do. *But as soon as we get him home to his parents, we have to find Abraham Lincoln,* he thought.

"Sam can sit in front of me and I'll hold on to him," Annie said to Jack. "You can take the reins and walk alongside us."

"Okay." Jack kept holding Sam, while Annie unhitched the straps, freeing the horse.

The wind had died down. The horse was calm as Annie coaxed her to a tree stump. She climbed onto the stump and then onto the horse's back.

"Your turn, Sam," said Jack.

Jack held Sam's elbow as the gangly boy climbed onto the stump. Then Sam hauled himself onto the horse in front of Annie. He started to slump forward. Before he could slide off, Annie grabbed him and held him up.

"Got him?" said Jack.

"My cornmeal," Sam whispered.

"I'll get it," said Jack. He found a panel in the

bottom of the grinder and opened it. Then he grabbed the empty sack and scooped the ground corn inside.

Jack slung the sack over his shoulder. Then he picked up the reins and turned the horse around. Annie held Sam as Jack led the horse along the lonely road back the way they had come.

This isn't the way things are supposed to happen, Jack thought. He knew they were supposed to trust the magic. But now they were helping the person who was supposed to help *them.*

"Where is your farm, Sam?" Jack asked after a while.

The boy didn't answer.

"Sam!" said Annie, giving him a little shake. "Your farm? Where is it?"

Sam opened his eyes. "Here," he said.

Jack didn't see any sign of a farm. The only things up ahead were a small, windowless log cabin and a shed. A curl of smoke rose into the white sky.

"Here *where*?" asked Jack.

Sam pointed to the cabin and shed.

That's it? Jack thought. *Sam's family must be really poor.*

The cabin and shed were in a scrubby clearing. The clearing was dotted with piles of stones and stumps where trees had been chopped down.

Not much of a farm, Jack thought. But at least they hadn't wasted a lot of time getting Sam home.

Jack led the horse toward Sam's farm. The cabin not only had no windows—it didn't even have a door! A black bearskin hung over the entrance. The horse stopped near the lean-to shed. The sound of a cow mooing came from inside.

"I'll help you, Sam," Jack said, dropping the sack of cornmeal to the ground. "Careful, careful."

Sam lowered himself down from the horse. When his feet touched the ground, Jack grabbed him. "Lean on me," he said. He put Sam's arm around his shoulders.

"Got him?" said Annie.

"Yep," said Jack.

As Jack and Sam stumbled toward the cabin, Annie slid off the horse and tied her to a fence post beside the shed. Then Annie grabbed the sack of cornmeal. She ran to the cabin and pushed aside the bearskin, so Jack could help Sam inside.

No one was home. The only light in the one-room cabin came from daylight streaming through big cracks between the logs of the walls. A low fire burned in a fireplace, but the air was cold and damp. The floor was made of dirt, and the crude furniture was made of planks of wood and tree stumps.

"Thank—thank you, Jack," Sam said, breathing heavily. "You can just leave me right here." He took his arm from Jack's shoulders and crumpled onto the dirt floor. He curled up and lay shivering on his side.

This is not good, thought Jack.

"You can't lie on the dirt, Sam," said Annie. "Don't you have a bed?"

Sam pointed to a loft.

"We'll help you," said Jack.

Jack and Annie pulled Sam up from the floor. He put his arms around their shoulders, and they brought him to a row of wooden pegs that led to the loft. Sam managed to pull himself up the row of pegs. When he reached the top, he disappeared.

"Now what?" Jack whispered to Annie.

Sam moaned from the loft above.

"Poor kid," Annie murmured to Jack. "There's no one here to take care of him."

Jack didn't know what to do. He wanted to help Sam, but they still had to find Abraham Lincoln in the countryside before he returned to the White House. And he wasn't sure how long the magic would work.

Another moan came from the loft.

"We have to help Sam," Annie said decisively. She climbed up the wooden pegs. Jack followed. As he crawled into the loft, he had to be careful not to bump his head on the ceiling.

Light and cold air came through the cracks between the logs. Sam was lying on a bed of corn husks and dried leaves. His fingers were pressed against his head.

"Does your head still hurt?" asked Annie.

"Bad," said Sam. He kept pressing his forehead, as if trying to push away the pain.

"Where are your parents, Sam?" asked Jack.

"Pa's gone," Sam said hoarsely. His eyes were squeezed shut. "Went to Kentucky last month."

"Where's your mother?" asked Annie.

Sam just shook his head.

"Can you tell us where your mother is?" Annie asked.

"Dead. She's dead. She died last year," said Sam. He covered his eyes with his arm.

"Oh, no," said Annie.

"Is there anyone who can take care of you?" Jack asked. He couldn't imagine being so alone.

"My sister, Sarah," Sam said in a muffled voice.

"Where's Sarah now?" asked Jack.

"School," said Sam.

"When does she get home?" asked Jack.

"After dark," said Sam.

"After dark?" said Annie.

"Short days in December," said Sam.

December? thought Jack. When they'd landed at the White House, it had been March. Maybe Sam's head injury had confused him.

"We're not leaving you, Sam," said Annie, "not until Sarah comes home."

"Don't . . . have to stay," said Sam, wincing with pain.

"We know we don't have to," said Jack. "But we want to."

And he meant it.

CHAPTER EIGHT

Into the Rough

Jack and Annie huddled in the loft near Sam. As the wind whistled between the logs, Jack could feel the boy's sadness.

"Thank you," Sam said. "But I have to get up now—have to do chores—help Sarah."

"No, not now," said Annie. "Maybe Sarah can take care of your chores when she gets home."

"She'll be too tired," said Sam. "She has to walk a long way home. With Pa gone, she can't sleep—hears wolves and wildcats all night."

"Really? Are there wolves and wildcats around here?" said Jack.

"Plenty," Sam said. "I have to do my chores—" He tried to sit up.

"Not until you feel better," Annie said firmly. "You lie here and rest. *We'll* do your chores. Just tell us what to do. We'll be happy to do it. Won't we, Jack?"

"Uh, sure . . . ," said Jack. "What are your chores, Sam?"

Sam lay back and took a deep breath. "Split wood," he said, closing his eyes, "milk cow, get water from spring . . ."

Jack slipped the pencil and notebook out of his back pocket and wrote:

split wood
milk cow
get water from spring

"Where's the spring?" asked Jack.

"Just a mile away, through the rough," said Sam.

"The rough?" said Jack.

"No problem," said Annie. "Anything else to do?"

"Make corn bread, then do homework in speller book . . . ," said Sam.

Jack added to his list:

make corn bread
homework in speller book

"That's it?" said Jack.

"Yes," said Sam.

"Good. We can do that!" said Annie.

We can? thought Jack. *Milk cow? Make corn bread? And what's "the rough"?*

"Sam, where's the rough?" asked Jack.

But Sam had fallen asleep.

"Sam?" said Jack.

"Shhh, let him sleep," Annie whispered.

Jack nodded. He followed Annie down from

the loft and across the dirt floor. She pushed aside the bearskin, and they stepped out of the cabin.

"Why did you promise to do Sam's chores?" said Jack. "We don't know how to do all that stuff."

"It was the only way to keep him from trying to work," said Annie. "He really needs to rest. Don't worry. We can figure them out. What's first?"

Jack looked at their list.

"Split wood," he said.

"How hard could that be?" said Annie. "There's the woodpile. There's the ax." She strode over to a stack of wood in the front yard. An ax was sunk into a fat log.

Annie rubbed her hands together, then wrapped them around the ax's long handle. She pulled and pulled, but the ax didn't budge.

"Let me try," said Jack. Annie stepped aside. Jack gripped the handle and pulled as hard as he could. But the ax stayed in the log.

"Forget it," said Jack. "It's like trying to pull the sword from the stone."

Annie laughed. "I guess we're not meant to be king," she said. "So, what's next?"

"Milk cow," Jack read from his list.

"All righty," Annie said cheerfully. She led the way to the shed next to the cabin.

Inside the shed, a cow was eating hay and swishing her tail. A three-legged stool and a tin pail stood in the corner.

"You try first," said Annie.

"Me?" said Jack.

"I tried the ax first," said Annie.

Jack put the pail under the cow and moved the stool close to her. Then he sat down.

The cow gave Jack a look. Then she whipped him in the face with her tail.

"Oww!" said Jack. He leaned forward and stared at the cow's udder.

Jack looked up at Annie. "I have no idea what to do," he said.

Annie laughed again. "Me neither," she said. "We'll come back to this, too. What's next?"

Jack jumped up from the stool and looked at

their list. "Get water from the spring," he said.

"I saw two jugs by the door," said Annie. "I'll get them." She ran to the cabin and came back a moment later with two brown jugs.

"Heavy," Annie warned. She gave one to Jack.

The jug *was* surprisingly heavy. "They'll be heavier with water," said Jack. "This isn't going to be easy, since the spring is a mile away, 'through the rough.' Whatever that means."

"I'll bet that's the rough over there," said Annie. She pointed to the woods on the other side of the clearing.

Jack and Annie wound their way through the stumps and stone piles until they came to the woodsy area, thick with underbrush. Wild grapevines twisted through bushes and around bare branches of small trees, binding it all together.

"It looks rough all right," said Jack.

Annie pointed to a narrow path. "I'll bet that's how to get to the spring," she said. "Want to give it a try?"

"Sure," said Jack. "Let's go."

Carrying the jugs, Jack and Annie started down the path. They pushed aside tangled vines and branches. Crows, sparrows, and woodpeckers swooped overhead. Squirrels ran up and down the small, bare trees.

Down the path, the rough got rougher. The path nearly disappeared. The tangle of undergrowth was so thick that Jack began to lose what little hope he had.

"I can't see pushing our way through this stuff for a whole mile," he said.

"Me neither," said Annie. "Let's go just a little further and see if it opens up again."

Jack and Annie pushed past more brambles and vines. "This whole journey is leading nowhere," Jack grumbled. "No spring water, no split wood, no cow's milk. Worst of all, no Abraham Lincoln. We've missed our only chance to use the magic to have a private meeting with him."

"I know," said Annie. "But we couldn't just leave Sam to try to do his chores. Offering to help him was the right thing to do."

"I know," said Jack.

"It's weird," said Annie. "Even though helping Sam isn't part of our mission, I feel like doing one good thing is somehow connected to doing another good thing. If we're helping Sam, we're also helping Penny."

"Yeah . . . ," said Jack. Despite his worries, he agreed with what Annie said. "There's only one problem: we have to get this feather from—"

"Yikes!" said Annie.

Jack looked back at her. "Yikes, what? You forgot we had to get a feather?"

"No. Yikes, did you hear that?" she whispered.

"Hear what?" whispered Jack. He held his breath and listened.

"A growl," whispered Annie.

Jack looked around, his heart pounding. "Like, uh—a wildcat growl? Or a wolf growl?" he asked.

"Like—*that* growl," said Annie.

Jack heard the long, low growl. He heard twigs breaking. The hair went up on the back of his neck.

CHAPTER NINE

Corn Bread and Molasses

"Turn around slowly," Jack said to Annie.

Clutching the water jugs, Jack and Annie turned around and started back the way they'd come. They tried not to make noise, but sticks and branches cracked and snapped.

The growl came again. *Louder.*

"Forget slow!" said Jack. "Run!"

Annie bolted ahead through the brush. Jack ran after her. His heart pounded. Brambles and vines blocked their way. Thorns snagged their clothes. They ran as fast as they could, not knowing if all the breathing and thrashing sounds were coming from them—or from the beast chasing them.

They burst into the clearing. Jack looked back. He didn't see a wolf or wildcat, but he wasn't ready to stop yet. "Keep going!" he cried.

Jack and Annie tore across the scrubby clearing. Finally they came to the cabin.

Sam was standing by the woodpile, swinging the ax! He gracefully split a log in two. He looked up at Jack and Annie and smiled. "How do?" he said.

Jack and Annie laughed as they tried to catch their breath. For some reason, Jack felt safe now, with Sam. "Fine!" he said. "Fine, fine, fine!"

"How do *you* do?" said Annie. "Why are you splitting wood?"

"I said to myself, I ain't going to lie in bed forever," said Sam. "My headache stopped as soon as I started my chores. I figured the two of you had left."

"Oh, no, we tried to do your chores," said Jack. "But—"

"We were headed to the spring to get water and we heard a growl," said Annie.

"Like a wolf," said Jack.

"Or a wildcat," Annie said.

"So we ran," said Jack.

Annie held up a jug. "No water. Sorry."

"No milk, either," said Jack.

"No split wood," said Annie.

"No corn bread," said Jack.

Sam gave them a big grin. "Don't worry. I took care of milking the cow, and I found water in the rain bucket. The corn bread's baking now."

"Wow," said Annie.

"That's amazing," said Jack. Now that Sam was better, he wondered if he could lead them to the president. "Do you still have time to help us find Abraham Lincoln?" he asked.

"Sure," said Sam. "I gave you my word."

"Great. Do you think he's still riding his horse in the country?" said Jack.

"Nope. He's not riding anymore," said Sam.

"But I guarantee you he's around here."

"Like where?" said Jack.

"Don't worry. I'll introduce you to him very soon," said Sam. "Let's go inside first."

Sam stuck his ax in a log. He picked up an armload of wood and headed into the cabin. As Jack and Annie followed, Jack glanced at the sky. The sun would be going down soon.

Inside, Sam put more wood on the fire. Then he lit two oil lamps. "Would you like to have some corn bread with butter and molasses?" he asked.

"Oh . . . wow . . ." Jack didn't know what to say. He was desperate to look for Abraham Lincoln, but he was also *very* hungry.

"I'd love it!" said Annie.

"Me too," said Jack, relieved. "We'll eat fast. And then we can look for Abraham Lincoln, okay?"

"Yes indeed. But first, you-all sit down," said Sam.

Jack and Annie sat on small tree stumps that served as stools. Sam lifted the lid on a pot

hanging over the fire. The delicious smell of corn bread filled the air.

Sam moved the pot to the wood table. Then he sliced pieces of steaming bread and put them on wooden plates. He smeared butter and dark molasses over the bread and ladled milk from the pail into wooden cups.

Jack sipped the sweet milk and ate the hot, buttery corn bread. "Yum," he said. He thought it might be the best meal he'd ever had.

"You really worked hard after we left," Annie said to Sam.

"I like to make things nice for Sarah for when she gets home from school," the boy said.

"Do *you* ever go to school?" asked Jack, his mouth full.

Sam nodded. "Since Pa left, I stay here to watch over things and do chores. But Sarah comes home and shares what she's learned. I do home-work and everything."

"Have you lived here a long time?" Jack asked, looking around at the crude cabin.

"A few years," said Sam. "We came from Kentucky. Pa and I cut our cabin out of the wilderness. We chopped down trees to make a road. We rolled fifty logs to this site and put up these walls. Did it all by hand and all without nails."

"Whoa," said Jack. It sounded like work for the strongest men, he thought, but Sam couldn't have been more than seven or eight at the time.

"We did as best we could with the furniture," Sam said with a laugh. "Someday we'll do better."

"It's not bad," said Jack. He looked at the cabin with new eyes. It seemed like a miracle now—everything made by hand, without the help of machines or even nails.

"You make all your own food, too, don't you?" asked Annie.

"'Course," said Sam. "We have our crops, and Pa hunts for our meat, or he did when he was here."

"I wouldn't be a good hunter," said Annie.

"Me neither," said Jack.

"Me neither," said Sam. "I shot a turkey once. Then I took a good hard look at the bird. I was so taken with its beauty, I ain't pulled a trigger on a wild creature since. That's why we haven't had any meat since Pa left."

"Well, you do a great job making corn bread," said Annie.

"You sure do," said Jack. He took his last bite, finished his milk, and wiped his mouth on his sleeve. Okay. Now they had to look for the president. Through the cracks in the cabin, he could see it was getting darker.

"Did you get all your chores done?" said Annie.

"Nope. I ain't worked in my Dilworth speller yet," said Sam. "But I don't really consider that a chore. It's my favorite thing. You could say I have a great thirst for learnin'."

"So do we," said Annie. "What's your homework for today?"

"Annie," said Jack, trying to catch her eye.

"Hold on, I'll get the speller that Sarah brought me from school and show you." Sam crossed the room and scrambled up to the loft. "The lesson I studied this morning is parts of speech," he called down.

"We have to go," Jack whispered to Annie.

"We can't hurt his feelings," whispered Annie. "Just let him show us the speller."

"But we have a mission—" Jack started.

"Here it is!" said Sam, climbing down from the loft. He grinned at them and held up a tattered book. "Would you mind giving me a little test?"

CHAPTER TEN

Readin' and Writin'

"We don't mind," said Annie.

"Annie," said Jack.

But Sam opened the speller and handed it to Annie. "Parts of speech," he said.

"Okay," Annie said. "What is a conjunction?"

Sam bit his lip. "Let's see . . . a conjunction is a part of speech that joins words and sentences together," he said. "Some conjunctions are *and, but,* and *because.*"

"Perfect!" said Annie.

"Yes, perfect," said Jack. "Here's an example: Jack wants to leave, *but* Annie is ignoring him."

"Good example," said Annie. "What is an interjection?" she asked Sam.

"That's a part of speech that expresses a sudden passion of the mind," said Sam, "such as 'Alack!' or 'Alas!' or 'Fie!' "

"Good," said Annie, laughing, "except Jack and I don't use interjections like those. We express a passion of the mind by saying things like 'Oh, man!' or 'Oh, wow!' or 'Whoa!'"

"Yes, that's right," said Jack, glaring at Annie. "Like 'Oh, man, time is running out!' Or 'Oh, wow, the sun is going down!' Or 'Whoa, we have a mission to complete!' "

Annie laughed again. "Right, that's how we use our interjections," she said to Sam. "What else is in your book?"

"Spelling and grammar rules," said Sam. "And quotes from the Bible and fables."

"Cool," said Annie.

Sam closed his speller. "I only wish I had more books," he said. "Anyone who'll give me a book is my best friend. I'll walk miles to borrow it."

"Jack would, too," said Annie. "And Jack and I both love to write, too. Don't we?" She looked at Jack.

"Yes, we do," said Jack, sighing.

"Oh, I do, too!" said Sam. "Neither my pa nor my ma ever learned to write. But I love it. I write words in the dust or the sand, even in the snow. I write them in the dirt floor with a stick." Sam laughed. Jack couldn't help smiling. "Why, I write on wooden shovels with charcoal!" Sam leaned forward and said in a hushed voice, "But the *best* thing in the world to write with is my quill pen and my blackberry ink!" Sam's face glowed in the firelight.

"Oh, wow, you do love to write," said Jack. "So do I." Jack forgot about Abraham Lincoln for the moment. "I love to make up my own stories."

Sam smiled. "Me too," he said. "And now I

want to tell you-all a good one. I meant to tell you this before, but I got kicked in the head before I could. I'm kind of famous for playing pranks on folks. But the two of you don't deserve—"

Suddenly noises came from outside: rumbling and neighing.

"What's that?" said Annie.

Sam froze. Then he turned to Jack and Annie, his eyes wide. "A wagon!" he said. He jumped up and rushed to the entrance of the cabin and pushed aside the bearskin.

"Pa!" Sam shouted, and he disappeared outside.

"His dad's back?" said Annie.

She and Jack hurried to the doorway and peeked out. Four horses were pulling a wagon through the cold dusk. The rickety wagon was filled with kids and furniture.

They watched as Sam ran toward the wagon and the driver pulled the horses to a halt. Sam's pa jumped down from his bench and threw his arms around Sam. They hugged for a long time.

Then a woman stepped down from the driver's bench. Three children scrambled down from the back. They stood smiling and giggling beside her.

"Son, I want you to meet my wife and your new ma from Kentucky," Sam's pa said. "And these are her children and your new sisters and brother, Elizabeth, Matilda, and John."

Each kid said "howdy" in turn.

"Howdy, son," Sam's new ma said. "I've so looked forward to meeting you. Thomas is awful proud of you and your sister. He says you're a good reader and a good writer."

"We hear you're a good woodchopper, too!" said the boy named John.

"And you like to tell stories!" said the girl named Elizabeth.

"And play pranks!" said the girl named Matilda.

"We brought you some books!" John piped up.

"And a feather mattress!" said Elizabeth.

"And a washstand and some soap!" said
Matilda. "Come look!"

The children grabbed Sam. He laughed as they
pulled him toward the wagon and started showing
him all the things they'd hauled from Kentucky.

Jack smiled. Sam wouldn't be sad or lonely anymore, he thought. It made him feel happy to see such a good thing happen to Sam.

"Let's slip outside and hide in the shed," Jack said to Annie. "So we don't have to explain where we came from."

Jack and Annie pushed past the bearskin into the shadows of twilight. They crept into the cowshed and peeked out.

"Pa?" someone shouted. "Paaaa!!!"

Across the clearing, a girl came running. She wore a black cape with a hood.

"Sarah! My girl!" Sam and Sarah's father rushed forward and threw his arms around his daughter.

Sarah started sobbing.

Her father hugged her. "Don't cry, girl," he said. "I brought you a whole new family. We'll all take good care of each other now. Come on, let's go in, and you can meet everyone. You'll love them all, Sarah, I promise. I give you my word."

As everyone headed into the cabin, Matilda exclaimed, "My goodness, you built this by hand?"

"What a wonderful job you did," said Sam's new ma.

"It's going to get better," said Sam's pa. "We're going to make a real door, aren't we, boys? And we'll make a real floor with wood, patch the roof, and put mud in the chinks between the logs."

"Yes, sir," said Sam and John together.

Thomas held the bearskin for his wife and all the children. Then he followed them inside.

Jack and Annie could hear the sounds of happy conversation coming from the cabin.

"Wow, what a day to be with Sam, huh?" Annie said to Jack.

"Really," said Jack. "But what should we do now?"

"I don't know," said Annie. "I think Sam forgot us in all the excitement."

"Like when Tad forgot me under the bed in the White House," said Jack.

"Jack! Annie!" Sam came running out of the cabin, calling to them in the fading light.

"He didn't forget us!" said Annie.

She and Jack stepped out of the cowshed.

"We're here!" Annie called.

"I want to give you something!" said Sam. He

held up a quill pen and a small bottle. "I told you about these. The pen's made from the feather of a goose, and the ink's from the roots of a blackberry bush. I want you to have them."

"Oh, no, Sam," said Jack. "You keep them. You need them more."

"Take 'em," said Sam. "I want to thank you for staying by me when I was feeling poorly, and for trying to do my chores. Your kindness truly helped me."

"But we didn't do any chores, not one!" said Annie.

"You tried, though," said Sam. "And most important, you both love what I love most: readin' and writin'. Please." Sam handed Jack the quill pen and the ink bottle. "Use them to write something special."

"We will," said Annie. "I can carry them, Jack." He handed her Sam's treasures, and she put them into her apron pocket. "Thank you."

"You're welcome," said Sam. "And what I was going to tell you is—"

"Yes—" Jack started.

But before Jack could finish, a *WHOOSH* and a *ROAR* shook the earth, like a speeding train passing by. The ground opened, and Jack felt as if he were falling through space,

through a tunnel,

down through blackness,

into a world of daylight.

CHAPTER ELEVEN

Abe Lincoln at Last!

Jack and Annie looked around in a daze. They were under the trees near the tree house, standing in the same spot where they'd sipped the potion. The air was chilly but bright. A fresh breeze rustled the branches.

"The magic ended," said Jack, stunned. "It ended before we could complete our mission."

"I know," Annie said. "And we didn't get to say good-bye to Sam."

"I didn't even thank him for the quill pen and the ink," said Jack.

"I know. These were his treasures," said Annie. She held up the goose feather and the ink jar that Sam had given them.

"Wait, that's so weird," said Jack. "We're looking for a feather, and Sam gives us a pen made out of a feather—"

Annie gasped. "Look, Jack!" She pointed toward the carriageway.

A tall man in a dark coat and a high black hat was striding toward the grove of trees. He turned his head, as if he were searching for something.

"At last!" said Jack.

"Mr. President!" Annie called. She thrust the quill pen and ink bottle back into her pocket and ran toward Abraham Lincoln.

"Wait!" said Jack, running after her. "What'll we say?"

"We'll figure it out!" said Annie. "Mr. President!"

Abraham Lincoln turned and looked in their direction. He froze and stared at them, as if he were both astonished and afraid.

What's wrong with him? thought Jack. As they got closer to the president, Jack and Annie slowed to a walk. Abraham Lincoln kept staring at them as if they were ghosts.

"Hello, sir," Annie said shyly.

Jack was speechless.

The creases in the president's face gave him a deeply worried look. His gray eyes stared at them

without blinking. "So it *is* you," he said in a hushed voice. "Tad told me your names, but I could not believe it might really be you."

"What do you mean?" Annie asked.

"You don't know who I am?" he said.

"You're Abraham Lincoln," said Annie. "President of the United States."

"Yes, but I spent the day with you once long ago," said the president. "And you vanished, right before my eyes."

"We did?" said Annie.

"Outside our log cabin in Indiana," said the president.

"Indiana?" said Jack.

"Yes, it was the day my father brought my stepmother home—and my new sisters and brother."

"Oh . . . *oh!*" said Annie.

"What?" said Jack.

"You were Sam!" said Annie.

"You were *Sam?*" said Jack. He couldn't believe it.

The president nodded.

Annie laughed. "So when we told you we were looking for Abraham Lincoln, you played a prank on us and told us your name was Sam!"

Abraham Lincoln smiled. "I haven't seen you since that day so long ago," he said. "And you haven't changed at all. I don't understand. Are you angels? Are you a dream?"

Jack was too stunned to answer. *It wasn't long ago, it was today,* he thought. *Or—maybe not.* Time and magic were confusing things.

"We're just regular kids, not angels," said Annie. "But maybe you should think of it all as a dream—a dream with a little magic thrown in."

Abraham Lincoln nodded slowly. Then he smiled. "I remember you tried to do my chores," he said, "and you thought some wild creature was chasing you. And you told me that your interjections were 'Oh, wow!' and 'Oh, man!'"

"Right," said Jack, smiling.

"You also said you loved learning and you loved

to read," said the president. "And you loved to write stories."

"And you said you loved to do that, too," said Annie. "So you gave us these." She pulled the ink bottle and the quill pen out of her apron pocket. "These were yours once, remember?"

Abraham Lincoln stared at the ink bottle and feather pen. "Yes," he said. "I made them from blackberry roots and a goose feather."

"Oh, man," whispered Jack. For the first time it fully dawned on him that Sam—who was really Abraham Lincoln—had given them a feather! The rhyme was starting to make perfect sense!

"Why have you come back?" asked the president.

Now Jack knew exactly what to say. "We have to give you a message of hope," he answered. He reached for the notebook in his pocket.

"Jack's right," said Annie. "Just a second." She opened the ink bottle and dipped the goose-feather pen into the ink. Then she handed the pen to Jack. "What should we say?" she whispered.

"Well, the Civil War is going to have a good ending," Jack whispered back. "All the country will come together."

"With freedom for everybody," whispered Annie.

"I'll write something about all that," said Jack. He thought for a second, and using the goose-feather pen, he scratched a message on a page in his notebook:

Never lose hope. This land will live
peacefully as one nation one day,
with freedom for everyone.

"You told us to use your quill pen and your blackberry ink to write something special," Jack said. He tore out the page and handed it to the president of the United States. "This is it."

Abraham Lincoln read the words on the paper. When he looked at Jack and Annie, the creases in his face had softened. His eyes

Mary Pope Osborne

had grown bright. "Oh, wow," he said softly.

Jack and Annie laughed.

"Do you really think so?" the president asked. "Do you promise?"

"Yes. I need to add something," said Jack. He took the note back from the president and wrote:

We give you our word.
—Jack and Annie

A shout came from the distance: "Pa! Pa!"

It was Tad. He was running up the carriage-way, with Willie right behind him.

"Mr. President, we have to leave now," said Jack.

"Really?" said Abraham Lincoln. He looked sad for a moment. Then he looked at his boys running toward him. "Yes, of course, I understand," he said.

"We'll never forget our times with you, Sam," said Annie.

"Nor will I forget," said Abraham Lincoln.

The boys were getting closer.

"Here, sir," said Jack. He gave the note back to the president. Then he and Annie started moving away.

"Good-bye!" they called to Abraham Lincoln.

The president waved and put their note in his pocket.

Then Jack and Annie quickly climbed up the ladder. Inside the tree house, they looked out the window. They saw Abraham Lincoln hurrying to meet his boys. When he caught up to them, he wrapped his arms around them both. They were all laughing.

"Abraham Lincoln's a good dad," said Annie.

"Yeah," said Jack, smiling. "Well, we'd better go now. Before Tad tries to take the tree house away from us."

Annie laughed. "He'll be pretty surprised when he discovers it's disappeared," she said. She picked up the Pennsylvania book and pointed to a picture of the Frog Creek woods. "I wish we could go home!" she said.

The wind began to blow.

The tree house started to spin.

It spun faster and faster.

Then everything was still.

Absolutely still.

CHAPTER TWELVE

The Feather of Hope

A spring breeze was whispering through the trees. "We're home," said Jack. They were back in Frog Creek, wearing their own clothes again. Jack looked in his backpack and pulled out their book on Abraham Lincoln.

Annie reached into one of her jacket pockets. "Good, they're still here!" she said. She took out Abraham Lincoln's gifts: the bottle of blackberry ink and the goose-feather pen.

"Cool," said Jack.

"Before we go, I want to look in our book and

see if there's a picture of Willie and Tad," said Annie. She took the book from Jack and checked the index. "Yes!" Then she turned to a page on the Lincoln children.

Annie read for a moment, then she whispered a sad "Oh, no." She closed the book and put it down. She looked terribly sad.

"What's wrong? What did you read?" said Jack.

"I just read that Willie died of typhoid fever in 1862," said Annie.

"Oh, no," said Jack. "That was the year after we met him."

"Poor Abraham Lincoln," said Annie.

"Poor Tad," said Jack.

"Yeah, he really needed Willie," said Annie.

"And then Tad will lose his dad just four years later," said Jack. "President Lincoln will get assassinated."

"I know," said Annie softly.

Jack didn't know what to say. He felt like the wind had been knocked out of him. All his annoyance at Tad disappeared. He wished he'd been kinder to him.

"It doesn't make sense, does it?" said Annie.

"I guess that's why *hope* is such an important thing," Jack said.

"What do you mean?" said Annie.

"We can't explain why sad things happen," Jack said. "All we can do is hope they make sense someday."

"Like when?" said Annie. "When will they make sense?"

"I don't know when," said Jack. "Maybe not even in a person's lifetime. Maybe in a world beyond this world." He sighed. "Maybe we just have to accept that it's a mystery."

Annie nodded, blinking back tears. "Well, we brought back the feather of hope," she said.

"And we gave hope to Abraham Lincoln," said Jack.

"And he did really great things as president, didn't he?" Annie said.

"Yeah, and he was a great dad, too," said Jack.

Jack placed the feather of hope in the corner of the tree house next to the glacial buttercup and the emerald rose.

"There's one more thing to get to save Penny," said Annie.

"Tomorrow," said Jack.

"Definitely," said Annie. "Today I just want to live my normal life: have breakfast with Mom and Dad—"

"And go to school," added Jack.

"We're lucky we can go to school," said Annie.

"Yeah," said Jack. "And we're lucky to have a nice house with heat and running water."

"And comfortable beds," said Annie. She started down the rope ladder.

"And lots of books," said Jack. He grabbed his backpack and climbed down after her.

As Jack and Annie headed home between the trees, a breeze shook the wet branches. Sparkling raindrops filled the Frog Creek woods.

Author's Note

When researching Abraham Lincoln, I was inspired by what his friends and family said about him. The sampling below taught me a lot about what kind of person he was.

From Dennis Hanks, Abraham Lincoln's cousin:

"Abe was getting hungry for books, reading everything he could lay his hands on. . . . He would go to the cupboard, snatch a piece of corn bread, take down a book, sit down in a chair, cock his leg up as high as his head, and read."

"[Abe] would commence his pranks, tricks,

jokes, stories, and . . . all would stop—gather around Abe and listen."

From Sarah Lincoln, Abraham Lincoln's stepmother:

"Abe was a good boy . . . was diligent for knowledge . . . and if pains and labor would get it, he was sure to get it. He was the best boy I ever saw. He read all the books he could lay his hands on."

"When he came across a passage [in a book] that struck him, he would write it down on boards if he had no paper and keep it there till he did get paper—then he would rewrite it, look at it [and] repeat it."

"Abe never gave me a cross word or look, and never refused in fact, or even in appearance, to do anything I requested him."

From a family friend of the Lincolns':

"If there was any motto or slogan of the White House during the early years of the Lincolns' occupancy it was this: 'Let the children have a good time. . . .' When the president came into the family sitting room and sat down to read, the boys would rush at him and demand a story. Tad perched precariously on the back of the big chair, Willie on one knee. . . ."

Now I hope that *you* will do your own fact-tracking—and enjoy learning more in the Magic Tree House Fact Tracker: *Abraham Lincoln.*

MAGIC TREE HOUSE
FACT TRACKER
Abraham Lincoln

A NONFICTION
COMPANION TO
MAGIC TREE HOUSE #47:
Abe Lincoln
at Last!

Mary Pope Osborne and Natalie Pope Boyce

Track the facts about
Abraham Lincoln
with Jack and Annie!

Mary Pope Osborne

is the author of many novels, picture books, story collections, and nonfiction books. Her *New York Times* number one bestselling Magic Tree House series has been translated into numerous languages around the world. Highly recommended by parents and educators everywhere, the series introduces young readers to different cultures and times in history, as well as to the world's legacy of ancient myth and storytelling. She and her husband, writer Will Osborne (author of *Magic Tree House: The Musical*), live in northwestern Connecticut with their three dogs. Ms. Osborne is coauthor of the companion Magic Tree House Fact Trackers with Will and with her sister, Natalie Pope Boyce.